Stone Soup

A Traditional Tale

Alison Hawes
Illustrated by Gwyneth Williamson

Once upon a time there was a man who liked to play tricks.

One day, the man came to a town.

On his cart, he had a big pot of water.

In his pocket, he had a small round stone.

The man said to the people,
"Stone soup. Stone soup for sale!"
The people laughed and said,
"You can't make soup from stones!"

4

"I can," said the man.

"I can make soup from this stone."

The people came to see him

make stone soup.

"First, I heat up a pot of water,"
said the man.
"Then I put in this small, round stone."

After a while, the man tasted the soup.

"**Mmmm**, it tastes good!" he said.

"If I had some onions,

it would taste better."

"Here are some onions,"
said an old woman.
The man put the onions in the soup.

After a while, he tasted the soup again.

"**Mmmm**, it tastes good!" he said.

"If I had some carrots,

it would taste better."

"Here are some carrots,"
said a young man.
The man put the carrots in the soup.

After a while, he tasted
the soup again.
"**Mmmm**, it tastes very good,"
he said.
"If I had some potatoes,
it would taste better."

"Here are some potatoes,"
said some children.
The man put the potatoes in the soup.

After a while, he tasted the soup again.

"**Mmmm**, delicious," he said.

"Can we taste the soup now?" asked the people.

"Oh, yes!" said the man.

The people tasted the soup.

"**Mmmm**," they said.

"This stone soup is delicious!"

The man sold all the stone soup.
Soon, he had lots of money.
Then he took the stone out of the pot
and put it back into his pocket.

He got into his cart.

"What a good trick!" he said.

"It always works!"

And he drove quickly away.